Jackie Chan

J. Poolos

The Rosen Publishing Group, Inc.
New York

Published in 2002 by The Rosen Publishing Group, Inc.
29 East 21st Street, New York, NY 10010

First Edition

Library of Congress Cataloging-in-Publication Data

Poolos, J.
Jackie Chan / by J. Poolos.— 1st ed.
p. cm. — (Martial arts masters)
Includes bibliographical references and index.
Summary: The story of action film star Jackie Chan, from his childhood as an indentured servant to the Peking Opera Research Institute, through his struggles finding his own style in Hong Kong cinema, to fame and fortune in Hollywood.
ISBN 0-8239-3518-3 (library binding)
1. Cheng, Long, 1954-—Juvenile literature. 2. Motion picture actors and actresses—China—Biography—Juvenile literature. 3. Martial artists—China—Biography—Juvenile literature. [1. Cheng, Long, 1954- 2. Actors and actresses. 3. Martial artists.] I. Title. II. Series.
PN2878.C52 P66 2002
791.43'028'092—dc21

2001004136

Manufactured in the United States of America

Table of Contents

Jackie Chan poses with the poster for his animated television series *Jackie Chan Adventures* during a Warner Brothers press tour.

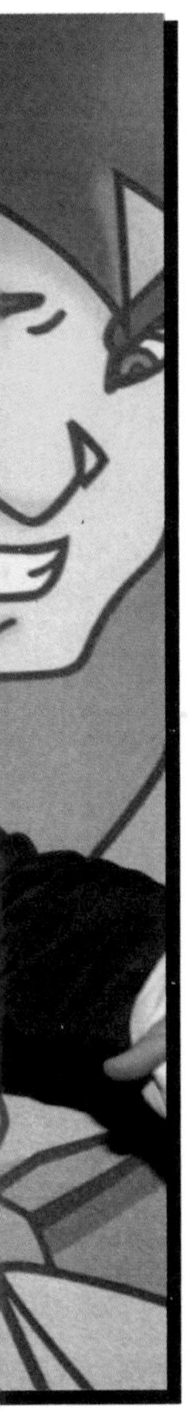

Introduction

For Jackie Chan, it has been a remarkable journey. Beginning with his early days at the Peking Opera Research Institute and his struggles as a junior stuntman, through his countless setbacks and his attempts to build a life in Hong Kong, Australia, and America, Chan has persevered. He has proven beyond all doubt that with a single-minded determination, a brilliant and creative mind, and a never-say-die attitude, a person who comes from humble beginnings can make it big.

His innovative style of fighting and slapstick interjections, which displayed an entire rethinking of martial artistry, caught audiences of action movies off guard. Although the fights are still at lightning speed and intensity, they make audiences laugh rather than groan and shudder. In Chan's battles, the hero doesn't so much defeat the villain as escape him or her through whip-quick evasive moves and feats of awe-inspiring physical dexterity. Instead of the classic martial arts weaponry, Chan uses whatever objects he can lay his hands on. His kung fu is for the common man, not the superman. Yet his amazing athleticism and eye for complex choreography make his art singular, fresh, and new. As the *South China Post* put it in a tribute to

Chan, "So successful was he that Chan can be said to have revitalized the entire Asian film business. Many producers and their stars tried to imitate Jackie's new genre of comedy kung fu, but all came to realize that Jackie Chan—like Bruce Lee before him—was one of a kind, inimitable."

Chapter 1

"Born in Hong Kong"

Most stories, even those of the greatest legends, begin with facts. Jackie Chan was born in Hong Kong on April 7, 1954, the Year of the Horse. He was the only son of Charles and Lee-lee Chan, who had recently fled the Japanese invasion of China. Charles and Lee-lee named their son Chan Kwong Sang, which means "Born in Hong Kong," to celebrate the family's safe arrival from mainland China. Chan weighed twelve pounds at birth, and his mother gave him the nickname A-puo, which means "Cannonball."

As the legend goes, Chan's parents were so poor they could not afford to pay the doctor for the surgery required during his birth. The doctor offered to "adopt" him to cover the costs of the medical bill. After careful consideration, Charles Chan declined the doctor's offer. They were poor for certain, but they would find a way to pay the bill so they could keep their only son. To them, Kwong Sang was a symbol of their new life. Charles Chan borrowed money from friends to pay the bill, and the Chan family went to live in the mansion of the French ambassador to Hong Kong. There, Charles Chan worked as a cook and Lee-lee Chan worked as a housekeeper.

A bustling street in Hong Kong around the time Jackie Chan was born

Times were tough for Charles and Lee-lee Chan. Both in their forties at the time of their son's birth, they lived hand-to-mouth on the low wages provided by the French embassy. But Charles Chan was often able to bring home choice cuts of meat and other foodstuffs from the embassy kitchen, and over the course of a few years, Jackie Chan grew into a healthy, active child. Because his parents worked long hours every day to provide their son with food and shelter, Jackie was left to do as he pleased. And what pleased him most was roaming the streets with friends, occasionally getting into trouble by picking fights. "When I was a child, I wanted to be a fighter, like Muhammad Ali," Chan once said.

The Peking Opera Research Institute

Realizing his beloved son might be headed for a life of dishonor, perhaps even danger, Charles Chan and a close friend took young Jackie to the Peking Opera Research Institute and enrolled him as a part-time student. There, Chan found a place among teachers and students who encouraged the physical behavior he craved. The institute was modeled after a traditional Chinese performing arts school and provided Jackie with an entrée into the ancient arts of acting, singing, dancing, and, most important, acrobatics and martial arts. Chan thrived at the school, which served as an outlet for his antics and enabled him to interact with kids his age in a supervised and productive environment. "I loved it," he remembered. "I

A performance by the Peking Opera. Jackie Chan was introduced to the martial arts when he studied at the Peking Opera Research Institute.

was able to kick and punch and do anything I wanted." It all seemed too good to be true. In fact, it was. Jackie Chan was about to learn some important life lessons as well.

When Charles and Lee-lee Chan were offered better jobs at the Chinese embassy in Canberra, Australia, they were forced to make a difficult decision. The new jobs presented the

Fun Fact

A huge singing sensation throughout Asia, Jackie Chan reportedly sang the title track for the Hong Kong release of the film *Beauty and the Beast*.

—*Time Out New York*
February 21–28, 1996

opportunity to make a more comfortable living, and they jumped at the chance to crawl out from under the dark cloud of poverty. Although both wanted their son to accompany them, they knew in their hearts that he had arrived at the age to begin his formal schooling. So, at the age of seven, Chan was indentured to the Peking Opera Research Institute. His new master, Sifu Yu Chan Yuan, paid a token sum to Charles and Lee-lee Chan to "adopt" the boy. As a part-time student, Chan had been perfectly happy. "When we went to sign me up, I was asked if I wanted to join for three, five, or ten years. At that age I had no concept of time, so I just picked ten." So began the training regimen that would make the son of impoverished parents into what some have called the biggest film star of modern times.

Chapter 2

The Seven Little Fortunes

What Jackie Chan didn't know when he innocently signed up for the ten-year program would shortly become clear: Once indentured, he became, in effect, a slave of the Peking Opera Research Institute. Chan has said that attending the school was almost like being in the army. The students had to wear uniforms of white tennis shoes and black pants. Worse, he was subjected to brutal beatings designed to break his will and his sense of identity.

Chan's routine at the institute was demanding. Every morning, he would awaken at five and start training immediately. He worked his voice; ran; practiced stick fighting, knife fighting, and sword fighting; worked on kicks; and practiced jumping, hapkido, judo, karate, and boxing. Often, he'd repeat more of the same training before the day was through.

The rigorous schedule was non-stop. To bed at midnight and up again at five, Chan's youth was hardly the stuff of the typical American kid. Each session would last two hours, and then he'd have to run to the next instructor for a different type of training. He didn't have time for anything but training.

Anyone who got tired from the day-to-day grind was punished in any number of ways that are considered abusive by today's standards. The boys were routinely threatened with physical punishment, starvation, and the withholding of privileges. Canings with bamboo sticks were a daily routine for most of the students. Land short on a jump or miss a dance step, and out came the stick. Beatings were something the students had to get used to. They had to just forget the pain and move on to the next training.

Students were also subjected to cruel endurance tests, including headstands for up to eight hours. Sometimes the teachers required students to assume the horse stance (where the legs are wide apart with the feet facing forward) while holding a bowl of water. If a student spilled even a drop, he or she was brutally beaten. Chan has often said he learned by the stick. "The stick told me when to jump, the stick told me when to kick. Other kids would do a trick and the sifu would say it was okay. Then I would do the exact same thing and be told to do it again. If I said I couldn't, he took out his stick and the stick would tell me I could."

The fact that his parents lived so far away did nothing to console Chan. While the other students' parents visited and sent gifts, he was on his own. At nights, while lying awake in the room where all the students slept, Chan dreamed of the day the harsh regimen, the beatings, and the loneliness would stop. What he didn't know at the time was that his hard work was about to pay off.

中正堂

Students training to be actors in Chinese classical theater go through a rigorous routine at the Peking Opera Research Institute. Chan once compared the training to military workouts.

Yu Chan Yuan, the school's strict master, placed Jackie in a student performance troupe called the Seven Little Fortunes. This troupe performed traditional Peking opera at various Hong Kong venues, giving Chan his first experiences performing in front of live audiences. Perhaps even more important, he bonded with two boys who would later have a significant impact on the Hong Kong film industry: Sammo Hung and Yuen Biao. The trio became known as the Three Brothers and would later team up in action films like *Winners and Sinners* and *Project A*.

Entering the Film World

But the good fortune didn't stop with the Seven Little Fortunes. In 1962, when Chan was just eight years old, a local director came to Yu Chan Yuan in search of a fresh young face for his film, *Big and Little Wong Tin Bar*. Not surprisingly, he chose Jackie Chan. Chan went on to appear in more than twenty films while he was a student at the school. By the time he was a teenager, he earned seventy-five dollars a day working as a stuntman. However, since he was still a student, he was required to turn over all of the money to his sifu, who would let Chan keep only a small fraction of what he'd earned.

Working on films and completing his training kept Chan busy during his final years at the institute, and before he knew it he had graduated. At the same time, film was increasingly replacing traditional Peking opera as a form

The Grandview Theater in the Chinatown district of San Francisco, California, showed Chinese films imported from Hong Kong during the 1960s, bringing American exposure to Chinese actors and stuntmen.

of entertainment in Hong Kong. Thus, the opera died as a popular art, and the film industry sprung up like a flower. Having spent the better part of ten years learning little else but performance techniques, the students of the institute, including Chan and his "brothers," were forced to switch gears and find stunt work in the action-oriented film business. Of course, this fit right in with Chan's plans. He dreamt of stardom, and he went to work at once fulfilling his dream of becoming a top-notch stuntman and fight-scene choreographer.

Today, Chan attributes much of his success to his sifu. Without the strict master, he would never have learned the martial arts and acrobatic skills on which his success depends.

"My sifu was a very good teacher and he taught me a lot. He trained my mind as well as my body," Chan said in an interview. "But I have paid back what I owe to him. All my creativity for choreographing fights comes from those years of training. All the things I use in my movies I learned from the school. But I would never put my kids, or any kids, through it. It's just too much."

The years of long hours, rigorous schedules, and brutal beatings would now pay off for a young Jackie Chan. Although he had learned little about reading and writing, he took what the school gave him and made it into something bigger than anyone at that time could possibly have imagined.

Chapter 3

Finding His Way

At seventeen years of age, Jackie Chan was a free man. No longer indentured to the Peking Opera Research Institute, he could work wherever he wanted, and for the first time in his life he was free to keep all his wages. On the other hand, for the first time in his life he had no home and no "family." Charles Chan called his son and asked him to move to Australia to be with him and Lee-lee. He promised a wealth of opportunities for employment and a roof over his head for as long as he needed. But Jackie Chan didn't want to go to a country where he would be a foreigner. Knowing the importance of contractual commitment in his parents' system of honor, he lied to his father, telling him he had secured a contract as a stuntman at a movie studio. Charles conceded, urging his son to honor the contract at all costs and to consider a move to Australia once the contract had expired. In a most gracious gesture indicative of his kindness, Charles then scraped together his hard-earned savings and purchased an apartment for his son. It was an act of kindness his son would never forget, for now he had a place to live, no matter how tough things got. And they would get tough.

Chan got right to work finding small film roles, taking whatever he could get and accumulating acting experience a frame at a time. He reportedly earned sixty dollars per stunt and, because he was just starting out, was obligated to return twenty dollars per stunt to the director. Having been so thoroughly trained in school, the stunts, fighting sequences, and acrobatics came easy to Chan, and it wasn't long before he began to turn his attentions toward establishing a reputation as a fearless performer.

But it wasn't easy. As a junior stuntman, Chan's specialty was playing dying characters. While senior stuntmen were leaping off buildings and crashing through plate glass windows, Chan practiced lying perfectly still. This was nothing

Jackie Chan began his professional movie career by
taking bit parts and proving himself as a stunt perfo

short of humiliating for the ambitious star-to-be, and he decided to do whatever it took to gain more respect as a stuntman.

While working at various studios in Hong Kong, Chan fell into a fraternity of stuntmen who lived every day as if it were their last. A wild and rugged bunch, they risked their lives by day and stayed up late into the night drinking, telling stories, and fighting. These men had a philosophy that described their style of living, and anyone who wanted to earn their respect would have to adopt it. It was called *lung fu mo shi*, or "dragon tiger." Chan has described the philosophy like this: "Power on top of power, strength on top of strength, bravery on top of bravery. If you were lung fu mo shi, you laughed at life before swallowing it whole." Stuntmen were lung fu mo shi when they did an amazing stunt or, better yet, when they tried a dangerous stunt and failed, then got up smiling and tried it again.

Chan threw himself into his work, giving everything to prove to stunt coordinators and directors that he could do anything. He volunteered to test difficult stunts, and when even the most fearless senior stuntmen balked at perilous stunts, he stepped forward to show them all it could be done. Before long, he had proven himself as a full stuntman, making more money and leaving the dying scenes to the junior stuntmen.

Meanwhile, Sammo Hung, Chan's "big brother" from the opera institute, had moved through the ranks to a position of stunt coordinator at the fledgling Golden Harvest studio. Hung consistently provided Chan with stunt work. But it was one of Chan's "big sisters" through whom he landed his first lead role, in a low-budget independent film called *Little Tiger of Canton*. Unfortunately, the director was disorganized. The equipment was poor. The script was unimaginative. And by the time the film was half-finished, the studio went broke. Chan's respect for directors hit a new low, and his dream of being a martial arts star was crushed.

Golden Harvest, however, was going strong. In 1970, Shaw Brothers Studios executive Raymond Chow had left the studio to start Golden Harvest, which he hoped would be a major distributor of independent films. Soon there was a big buzz around the industry about a certain actor Chow had discovered. The actor was a United States–born Chinese man who had earned a strong cult following while playing a supporting role in an American television series. The series was *The Green Hornet*, and the actor was Bruce Lee.

Bruce Lee

As a martial arts actor, Lee was unique. His fighting style was bare, quick, and brutal. His on-screen presence was intense to the point of discomfort. At a time when it was traditional for martial arts actors to play noble characters, Lee played delinquents. He was perfect at portraying the loner who used

Seeing Bruce Lee at work during the filming of *The Chinese Connection* (originally released as *Fist of Fury* in Hong Kong) spurred Jackie Chan's desires for international stardom.

his fists to solve problems. His first film with Golden Harvest, *The Big Boss*, took Hong Kong and all of Asia by storm, and catapulted the studio to the top of the industry.

One day in 1973, Sammo Hung called Chan with an offer to play a stunt role in *Fist of Fury*, in which

Bruce Lee was to star. Directed by the infamous Lo Wei, *Fist of Fury* (known to American audiences as *The Chinese Connection*), would make Lee an international star and the biggest name in the history of kung fu movies. Chan played a bit role as one of the many fighters Lee defeated, but he was able to witness firsthand what made Bruce Lee such a legend. Chan found the star to be an intense figure both on and off the set. But he was kind and encouraging as well. Chan still remembers two things he learned from Lee. First, he saw in Lee a man who wanted to change the world. That taught Chan the importance of having great ambition, which he would use as motivation for the years to come, as he became a major figure in the film industry. Second, Chan saw Bruce

Lee as a real man, not as a god or a mythical character. Certainly he deserved admiration. But unlike so many hangers-on around the set, Chan stopped short of worshiping Lee. He thought if Lee could achieve so much, there was no reason he couldn't do the same. Soon, however, he would find out just how difficult it was to become a star.

It was during the filming of *Fist of Fury* that Chan met Willie Chan, then working with the Cathay Organization, another Hong Kong studio specializing in action films. Jackie had just completed a stunt that left him lying flat on his back, the breath knocked out of him. As the director signaled a wrap for the day, Chan remained on the ground, tired and in pain, gathering his strength to get up and go home. Willie Chan came over to compliment his work, left his card, then ducked out the back door. Jackie didn't know it then, but Willie Chan would come into his life later in a very important way.

Shortly after *Fist of Fury* was finished, Chan left his old friend Sammo Hung and Golden Harvest studio to take his first job as stunt director. It was a big move up, and he jumped at the opportunity. At Da Di Studio, he worked on two low-budget films, *The Heroine* and *Police Woman*. Both were critical and financial flops, and although Chan was gaining great experience as a stunt coordinator, when the studio finally closed its doors he was left out on the street, unpaid, broke, and unemployed.

With his options played out in the competitive Hong Kong film industry, Chan called his father for help. Shortly thereafter, he packed his bags and left Hong Kong to live in Australia. For Chan, it was the beginning of an era that would show just how tough he was, not only as a stuntman who punished his body and risked his life on a daily basis, but as a young man with great ambition. In the next few years, Jackie Chan would find out what he was made of.

Chapter 4

A Test of Character

With no small degree of humility, Chan set foot on foreign soil. For the first time in his life he was an outsider. His physical features made him stand out against the backdrop of very Western-looking Australians. He was used to customs and manners that were entirely different. He didn't speak a word of English. And although he was happy to see his parents for the first time in fifteen years, every moment in Australia was a struggle. After only a few months in his new country, he swallowed his pride and called Sammo Hung to ask for a job in Hong Kong. Always the big brother, Hung got Chan a job on John Woo's first film. Woo has since become a legend in both Hong Kong and Hollywood as a director of high-flying action movies.

In *Hand of Death*, Chan performed stunts and played a small supporting role. Once the shooting wrapped, he fully expected to be back in the thick of things in Hong Kong, getting stunt roles and occasionally playing bit parts. But it was not to be. Times were tough for everyone in the action film genre. Even the well-established Hung was worried about keeping his job. But why had a thriving industry so suddenly fallen

The Next Bruce Lee?

After Bruce Lee's untimely death, many Hong Kong martial artists tried to take his place. Some even used names like Bruce Le and Bruce Li! Of course, no one was able to replicate his skill and style, so many Hong Kong action movies flopped. Many said it was the death of the genre.

on hard times? Ever since Bruce Lee's tragic death in 1973, action movies weren't drawing the big audiences necessary to keep the studios in the black. Comedy had become the genre of choice for Hong Kong audiences, and as a result stunt work was drying up. Golden Harvest bore the brunt of this change in interest, and the studio could not offer Chan additional work. Once again broke and unemployed, he borrowed money to buy a ticket to Australia. He returned to his parents' home, fully resigned to retirement from the film industry and committed to making a life in Canberra, Australia.

On Foreign Soil

Once again Chan was a foreigner. But he was willing to work hard to fit in. He acquired an Australian passport and did odd jobs to earn his keep. By night he assisted his father as a cook at the embassy. By day he was a construction worker. His boss at this job was the one to give Chan, who still went by Kwong Sang but who had had many different stage names, his now-famous nickname. When the other workers wanted to know Chan's name, Jack—the boss—thought Kwong Sang would be too hard for them to remember, so he said, "His name is Jack, too."

Chan enrolled in English classes, fully intending to master the language. But he was unhappy sitting in class. He felt the need to be fighting, falling, and tumbling, and neither the classes nor his work provided him with this much-needed outlet for the action and activity on which he thrived. Sad and disillusioned, he went about the monotonous business of life with a homesickness for the movies.

His mother consoled him, telling him she knew he was destined for great things and that he must be patient in letting those good things come to him. As fortune had it, the stroke of good luck was right around the corner. A few months after his arrival in Australia, when he felt the most down on his luck, he got a phone call. It was Willie Chan, the director he had met on the set of *Fist of Fury*. Willie wanted Chan to star in Lo Wei's remake of *Fist of Fury*. Out of all the actors and stuntmen in Hong Kong, Jackie Chan had been pegged to play the lead role, standing in for Bruce Lee.

As part of the preparation for his leading role, Chan was treated to unexpected cosmetic changes. Lo Wei paid for a surgeon to perform a common operation that would widen Chan's eyes and make him appear more like a westerner. He also paid to have Chan's teeth straightened for the all-important close-ups. As a final step, he gave Chan the stage name Sing Lung, which translates to

Kung Fu

At the Peking Opera Research Institute, Jackie Chan had been schooled in a variety of martial arts forms. He was proficient using his hands and feet as required by traditional kung fu styles of both the north and the south of China. But through his experience working on films, he had trained in other styles and was a well-rounded martial artist. It should be noted that Chan is not a student of karate, the traditional Japanese martial art. His focus has been on kung fu, the martial art of China, "invented" by Shaolin monks almost 2,000 years ago.

Kung fu has more than 1,500 styles, each with different approaches to offense and defense, as well as different learning methodologies. In kung fu movies, many of the styles displayed by actors and stunt performers are derivative of the animal styles, which imitate offensive and defensive characteristics of the creatures after which they are named. Here are just a few of the styles you'll see in kung fu films:

Dragon: The master of the dragon style uses ch'i rather than physical force to defeat or subdue his or her opponents. (Ch'i is the vital force of life. The term comes from the Chinese word for "breath.") Ch'i is akin to a spiritual magic. In films, this style is exemplified by the martial artist flying and exhibiting other supernatural powers.

Crane: The master of the crane style uses his or her feet and legs to fend off attackers. He or she stands on one leg, with the other leg lifted and bent, often with the arms reaching upward. The actions of the hands imitate the beak of the crane, making quick, darting motions.

Snake: Using this offensive and comparatively brutal style, the martial artist emphasizes the fingers, using them to strike at the upper portion of the opponent's body (usually the face and throat). Unlike the similar cobra style, the martial artist does not grab and clench to the death, as a snake would strike and hold on. He or she merely uses fast, fluid motions to strike at an opponent.

Tiger: The master of the tiger style employs powerful kicks and vicious clawing motions that will tear at the flesh of an opponent. Two features of this style are the tiger claw, a hand pose that defends against weapons, and the powerful movements of the arms and legs.

Choi Li Fut: This style relies on power and features short, choppy movements. The martial artist assumes what is called the riding horse stance, with his or her feet at shoulder width, knees bent. With quick, powerful chopping motions, the martial artist blocks attacks and lunges in for offensive strikes.

Drunken: A sub-style practiced by Chan in several of his films, the drunken style relies on lurching actions intended to wear an opponent down. The martial artist strikes at any exposed area with no obvious pattern. The blows are not particularly powerful or lethal but in time can be enough to exhaust an opponent.

Jeet Kune Do: Developed by Bruce Lee, this style is a mix of several other styles, including tai chi and jujitsu. The name translates to "intercepting the fist." The style requires flexibility and innovation and is most useful when fending off a dozen or more attackers.

"already a dragon." As the studio was preparing to begin filming, the stunt coordinator was injured while off the set. Chan seized the opportunity and stepped in to fill the role. That was when he learned his salary as a stunt coordinator well exceeded his salary as the leading man. Upon expressing his dismay to Willie Chan, the latter told him he was being paid as a novice actor and as an experienced stunt coordinator. That seemed to sit well with Chan, and he threw himself into both roles with an eye for stardom.

Still, Chan found filling in for the legendary Bruce Lee a daunting challenge. Lo Wei wanted Chan to be Bruce Lee, and this was hard for Chan to accept. He wanted to be himself, but that just wasn't in the cards. On camera, Lee was dark, grim, and intense. It just wasn't Chan's—or any other actor's—style. Chan was more comfortable with humor, the sillier the better. By then he had become a huge fan of Buster Keaton's silent movies and the Marx Brothers' comedies, and his instinct was to affect a style of hyper-animated fighting moves and to work slapstick comedy into his fight scenes from time to time. This didn't sit well with Lo Wei, and despite the frustration, Chan was forced to look and fight like Bruce Lee.

Yet it was an important realization for Chan. He hoped that after *Fist of Fury II* was finished he would have the opportunity to introduce the movie-watching public to his brand of martial arts. In a sense, it was the dawn of the Jackie Chan style.

Chapter 5

The Birth of the Jackie Chan Style

About fifty minutes into the blockbuster hit *Rumble in the Bronx*, Jackie Chan's character is attacked by a dozen or so bad guys. In traditional martial arts flicks, the hero would face his attackers and fight to the finish. But Chan turns on his heels and flees. What follows is an elaborate chase scene that ends when Chan jumps from a truck as it falls from three stories. This scene is typical of Chan's cinematic style, but it is also emblematic of his life at that time. Later in the movie, he advises another character: "Don't let the situation change you. You have to change it."

After *Fist of Fury II* was finished, Chan sat down with Willie Chan to discuss his frustrations with the direction of his career. Willie agreed that Chan was not suited for the Bruce Lee style of martial arts. But unlike Jackie, whose frustrations grew out of a dissatisfaction with his "art," Willie saw the bigger picture. He told his friend that he was gaining a reputation as a box office bust. If Jackie's string of bad movies continued, soon he wouldn't be hired at all. Willie Chan promised to help the career of his old friend.

Whatever it was that Willie did to help worked. Lo Wei signed

Ah Keung (Jackie Chan), coiled to strike against a street gang in *Rumble in the Bronx*

Chan up for *Half a Loaf of Kung Fu* and gave the emerging star more creative clout. This was Chan's chance to show the world what he could do. He worked with the film's director to make *Half a Loaf* like nothing anyone had seen before—a martial arts movie turned on its ear, with wild slapstick replacing the theme of revenge. Chan was proud and passionate about his work. Upon viewing the footage, Lo Wei was less excited. In fact, he was furious. Although Willie tried to explain Chan's approach to Lo Wei, even his words of support did nothing to soothe the narrow-minded producer. The film was shelved before anyone got the chance to judge for themselves.

Following the disaster, Jackie made *Spiritual Kung Fu,* a Lo Wei–directed comedy that was so bad Lo Wei could not convince industry executives to commit funds or support to distribute the movie. Lo Wei went back to the tried and true, directing Chan in *Dragon Fist*, another martial arts film where Chan acted and fought in the style of Bruce Lee. But by now Lo Wei had grown impatient with Chan's apparent failure as a box office sensation. Willie Chan had promised Jackie Chan would be a star, but it just wasn't happening.

The Jackie Chan Movie

But Willie had a plan. The fact that the overbearing Lo Wei was stifling Chan's creativity was not lost on the actor's friend. He arranged to loan Chan to Ng See-Yuen at Seasonal Films, a smaller competitor with a reputation for making high-quality films with no-name actors. What Chan found at Seasonal shocked him. Instead of immediately throwing him into a preestablished role in a traditional martial arts film, See-Yuen told him only Chan knew what Chan could do. See-Yuen wanted to know what that was, then they would go from there. For the first time in his

Fun Facts

- Jackie Chan was honored as the guest of the Chinese consul general in Los Angeles, California, in February 1996.
- Jackie Chan received the key to the city of Los Angeles in 1996.

long career, Jackie Chan was being consulted not only as an actor and stunt coordinator but as a filmmaker. He was ready with an answer. All the ideas he had been working on over the years came out like a flood. In his autobiography, *I Am Jackie Chan*, Chan recalls what he told See-Yuen that day:

> Bruce [Lee] was the best at what he did. No one can do it better. So why try? People want to see living ideas, not dead bones. Bruce was a success because he was doing things no one else was doing. Now everyone is doing Bruce. If we want to be successful, we need to do the opposite.
>
> Bruce kicked very high. I say we should kick as low to the ground as possible. Bruce screamed when he hit someone to show his strength and anger. I say we should scream to

show how much hitting someone hurts your hand. (Jackie held his hand and winced in mock pain.)

Bruce was Superman, but I think audiences want to see someone who is just a man, like them. Someone who wins only after making a lot of mistakes, who has a sense of humor. Someone who's not afraid to be a coward.

Chan waited for See-Yuen's response. He wondered if his "crazy" ideas would make much sense to a man as established as See-Yuen. To his surprise, See-Yuen agreed with him 100 percent. "Let's do it," he said. "Let's make your movie."

See-Yuen turned directing duties over to a former Peking Opera Institute student named Yuen Woo-Ping, who was making his directorial debut. Chan hadn't known this big brother, as Woo-Ping had left the school before Chan's arrival. But he knew he would be working with someone familiar with the teachings of their sifu, someone who knew exactly what he was capable of as a performer. Chan showed him some of the snake fist forms he'd been working on. The two agreed to base the film on this style and incorporate acrobatic stunts. As far as the plot was concerned, they conceived of an idea that was new to Hong Kong cinema: They would turn the master-student relationship upside down. The master would be portrayed as an old beggar, and the student would be a country bumpkin. This setup gave them freedom to invent new twists that would parody traditional teacher-student interaction. By the time they wrapped up the shoot, they realized they had made a truly unique martial arts film. Backing up their realization was the fact that *Snake in Eagle's Shadow* was a bona fide blockbuster.

Every day, See-Yuen, Woo-Ping, and Chan sat at a table poring over the box office numbers from the Asian market. One day See-Yuen asked them a question: "What's the biggest film in the history of Hong Kong?" *Fist of Fury,* Jackie replied. *Way of the Dragon* was bigger, said Woo-Ping. "You're both wrong," replied See-Yuen, a big smile spread across his face. "The correct answer is *Snake in Eagle's Shadow.*" Chan was elated. Bigger than Bruce Lee! Finally his star had arrived, just as his mother had promised it would.

With his next film, Chan had to prove to the film industry that the "Jackie Chan movie" was no fluke and that he was something more than a one-hit wonder. His answer was a story about the legendary Chinese hero Wong Fei-hung—doctor, healer, and one of the most

Wong Fei-hung (Jackie Chan) unleashes a punishing blow on a bad guy in *Legend of the Drunken Master*.

powerful martial artists of his time. Uncountable movies had described the life of this cult figure, who was central to the heart of all Chinese people. But Chan had his own ideas about how to truly portray the giant. His idea was to tell the story of Wong before he became the legendary master and to show the subject as a lazy, naïve, and rebellious youth. Thus, *Drunken Master* was born.

The film was a sensational hit. Audiences packed the theaters to see this ridiculous style of fighting and the humorous interpretation of a great historical figure. With the success of the film came fame. Instantly, Chan was recognized on the streets as a celebrity. Fans swarmed around him, begging for his autograph. And he was finally able

Jackie Chan, as the Drunken Master

to buy a new apartment, clothes, jewelry, and fancy dinners, which were part of the typical movie star's lifestyle. But his world was about to change yet again. Lo Wei wanted him back, and he was obligated by contract to make one more movie with the dictatorial director.

As usual, Lo Wei had a heavy hand in directing Chan's next endeavor, but both Jackie and Willie knew that Jackie's success was founded on his freedom to create. After several big arguments, Jackie was permitted to direct his first feature. It was a huge opportunity for him, a directorial debut. He poured everything into the film, and *Fearless Hyena* was his biggest box office score thus far. It was also Lo Wei's biggest moneymaker since his films with Bruce Lee.

A bidding war for Chan's services soon ensued. Among the offers was one for more than $4 million to sign with Golden Harvest. Although other studios offered more, Willie encouraged Jackie to sign with Golden Harvest because it was a well-respected and established studio. As was his habit, Chan took the advice of his trusted friend and made a deal.

Golden Harvest gave Chan carte blanche, including unlimited budgets and few restrictions on timelines for the films on which he worked. Better yet, he had total creative freedom as long as he tried to break new ground with each feature. Chan's response to his boss's confidence was a look at classical kung fu called *The Young Master*. Meanwhile, while Chan was consumed with his new responsibilities, a desperate Lo Wei had called in

The Activist?

In 1992, Jackie Chan led more than 300 people to march on Hong Kong's police headquarters to protest the powerful local influence of Chinese organized crime, otherwise known as the Triad.

his gangster friends from the Hong Kong mafia, otherwise known as the Triad. The idea was to try to negotiate for Chan's return to work for Lo Wei.

If that failed, the Triad would use any force necessary. Chan went at once to Willie, who spoke to the executives at Golden Harvest. A negotiator was summoned to try to smooth things out, and Chan was sent to the United States until things cooled off in Hong Kong.

A Chance in Hollywood

Chan arrived in Hollywood and went straight to Golden Harvest's American offices. He went to work on a 1930s period piece called *Battle Creek Brawl*. He had only two weeks to learn his lines in English and to pick up roller-skating, which he would do in the movie. Excited for a shot to make it in Hollywood, Chan worked hard. But he found the directing style different from what

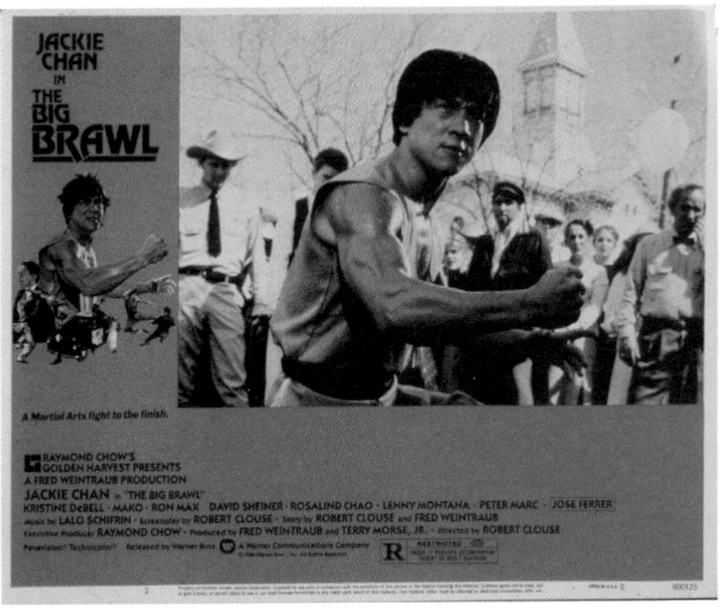

The Big Brawl (also known as *Battle Creek Brawl*) was Jackie Chan's first Hollywood movie.

he was accustomed to, and he thought there was too much footage of his character walking around. The American audience, he learned, wanted serious heroes.

As shooting wrapped up, he learned through Willie Chan that *The Young Master* was a hit. He was happy to know that Golden Harvest bought out his contract with Lo Wei Productions, and that after a few altercations involving the police, the negotiator had appeased the Triad. Things would go smoothly from here, he thought: A quick return to Hong Kong, then back to making movies.

But to his surprise, he was to appear in one more American picture, the star-studded *Cannonball Run*. Golden Harvest wanted to make Chan a hit in America, and they thought if he couldn't do it on his own, he would do it on the coattails of American stars like Burt Reynolds and Dean Martin.

At the time, no one recognized Jackie as Hollywood star material. His English was at best shaky, and, although his exaggerated facial expressions were humorous, Americans seemed to want more

Jackie Chan *(center)* poses with the cast of *Cannonball Run* at a promotional event in 1981.

sophistication in a leading role. Feeling like he had yet to get a fair shake in America, Chan returned once again to his homeland.

Chapter 6

Return to America

Chan was still smarting from what he thought was sub-par treatment by the American studios and press. Even though he had yet to make a name in the United States, he was Hong Kong's biggest star. He was stunned at how little that counted in America. With a blind determination, he got to work at once on *Dragon Lord*, a sequel to *The Young Master.* Meanwhile, he was living the life of a true star. Wherever he went, his

Jackie Chan as Dragon in *Dragon Lord*

entourage of stuntmen and hangers-on followed. He treated them to expensive Scotch and fine meals. And he showed no respect for authority. He was young, rich, and spoiled by fame.

Reacting to the casual attitude with which his American directors set up and shot scenes, Chan became a perfectionist. At least that was his intention. Not only did his film go over budget, but the shoot went several months past schedule. Part poor planning, part obsession with success, it led Chan to do more than 2,900 takes on a single scene. Still, *Dragon Lord* was a flop in theaters. Had Jackie Chan lost his magic?

The answer was probably no, but he had certainly lost his way. After another long talk with Willie Chan, he came to realize that with all the

Fun Facts

- Jackie Chan is a founder and officer of the Hong Kong Directors Guild, Performing Artists Guild, and Society of Cinematographers.
- When his studio could not get stuntmen and stuntwomen insured for his films, Jackie Chan founded his own association for stunt performers. He pays any medical bills out of his own pocket.
- Jackie Chan formed his own production company, Golden Way, which began producing films with Golden Harvest's Raymond Chow, notably *Rouge* (1988) and *Center Stage* (1992).
- Jackie Chan is the owner of Jackie's Angels, a casting and modeling agency.

time he had invested in pursuing his dream, he had neglected his heart, his friends, and those who had helped him when he was in need. It was a bitter pill to swallow. How could he have been such a jerk? And what could he do to get back on track?

The answer came immediately. He called his brothers Sammo Hung and Yuen Biao to invite them to work together. The trio came out with *Winners and Sinners*, which featured an ensemble cast that included some of China's biggest names in entertainment. Chan admitted to enjoying the shoot immensely, and to no one's surprise the movie was a hit. Jackie was back.

Because *Winners and Sinners* had been so much fun to work on, Chan wanted to continue working with Hung and Biao. He realized that they both needed their space and that they wouldn't want to go on forever being known as "Jackie Chan's brothers," but he wanted to keep a good thing going as long as everyone was comfortable.

The trio would go on to make seven movies together. But what followed *Winners and Sinners* was another breakthrough film. The three brothers worked together almost seamlessly. Each had his own strength and style: Hung was big and powerful; Biao was lithe and acrobatic; and Chan excelled at stunts. The result was *Project A*, a film that took action to a new level. Although the film succeeded because of the collaboration between the three brothers, it also marked the first time that Chan tried out the "really really really dangerous stunt" that has since become his signature.

The Price of Fame

"Twice a year, [Chan] hosts a party for the Jackie Chan International Fan Club, many of whose members fly in from Japan. At one point, the club had more than 10,000 members, most of them girls. Being a teen idol, however, has exacted its price: in his films and his private life, Chan must be careful not to reveal too much romantic involvement. In 1985, after he mentioned in an interview that he was dating someone, a Japanese girl committed suicide. [She threw herself in front of the Bullet Train.] The next year, another Japanese fan arrived at his office, announced her intention of bearing Chan's child and drank a vial of poison."

—From "Jackie Chan, American Action Hero," by Jaime Wolf, *New York Times Magazine*, January 21, 1996

In the film's showcase stunt, Chan was to leap onto a clock tower, hang from one of the clock's giant hands, fall more than fifty feet, crash through three awnings, and finally land on the hard ground. Every day for six straight days, Chan would hang from the clock's hand, trying with all his might to summon the courage necessary to make the fall. And every day he would have his spotter pull him back onto the ledge. Finally, he had had enough, and he made the leap. But it wasn't good enough. In order to get all the camera angles necessary to make the stunt absolutely awesome, he would have to perform the stunt three times, repositioning the cameras each try. As a result, *Project A* was a smashing success, and the three brothers were on a roll.

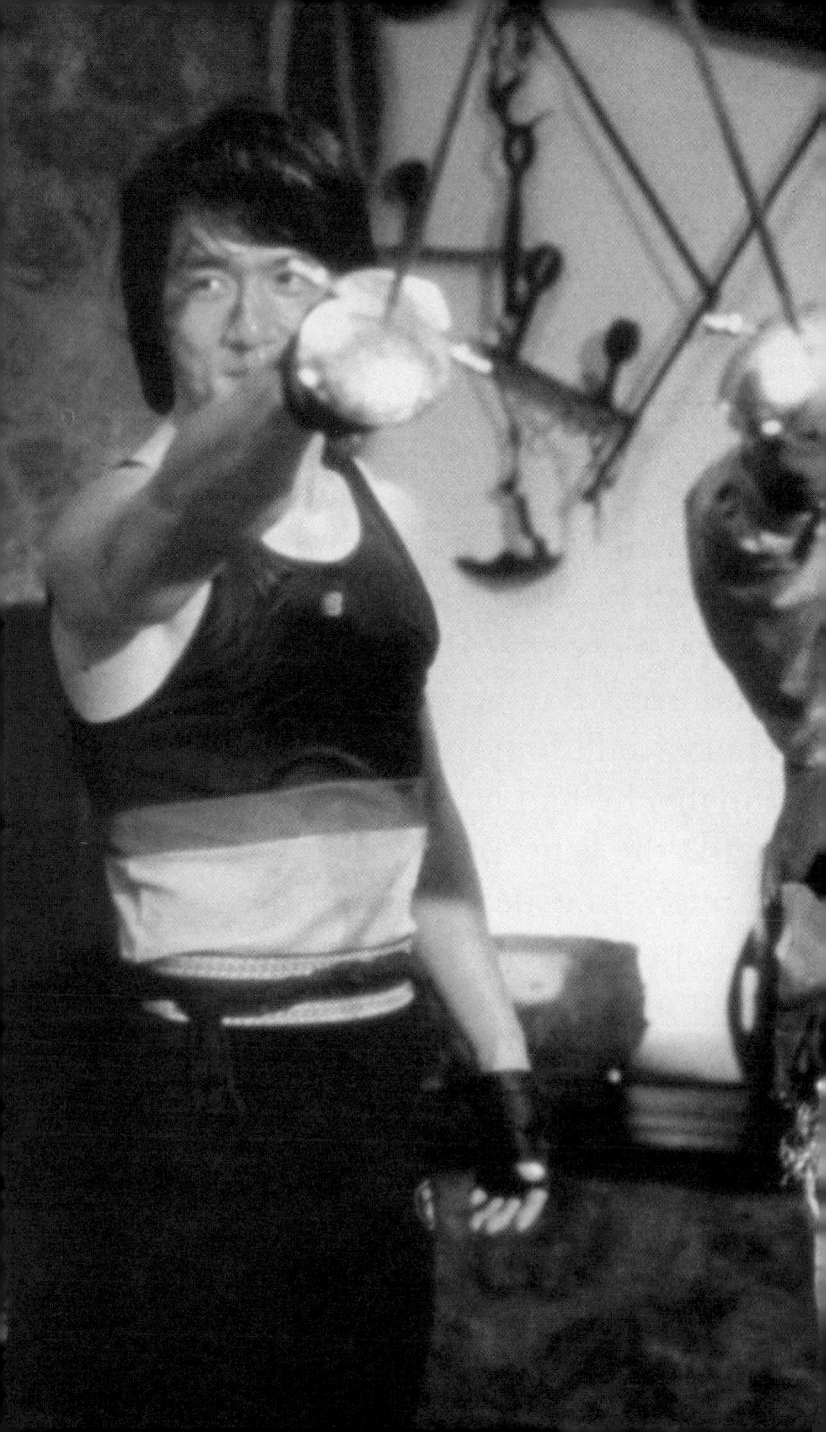

Jackie Chan *(left)* reunites with Sammo Hung *(center)* and Yuen Biao in the action comedy *Wheels on Meals*.

As the box office scores piled up, the studio became more and more generous with their funding. Golden Harvest gave the brothers $3.5 million for their next film. Hung, Chan, and Biao decided to shoot *Wheels on Meals* in Spain. It was time to take Hong Kong cinema to Europe. Chan had another hit on his hands, and Golden Harvest, satisfied that Chan still packed star power in the Asian markets, sent him back to America to try once again to break into the U.S. market.

Chan was cast in *The Protector,* with Italian American actor Danny Aiello. He was disappointed in director James Glickenhaus's haphazard approach to filmmaking. While Chan was used to spending twenty days or more to film a fight sequence, Glickenhaus took only four. Worried that the film would be a poor reflection on him, but powerless to do anything about it, he concentrated on the film's Asian release. With a controlling hand, he reshot the final fight scene with Aiello and the other cast members.

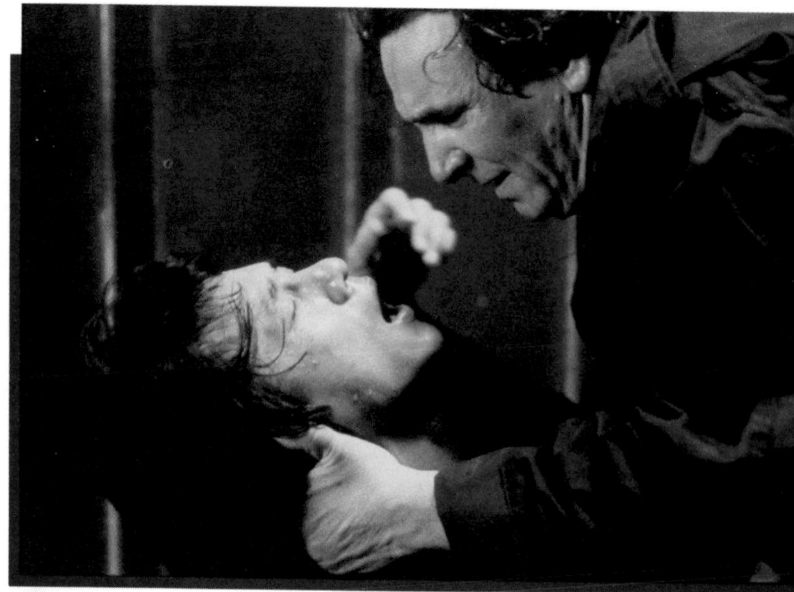

In *The Protector*, Jackie Chan and Danny Aiello star as New York City policemen who go to Hong Kong to investigate a drug lord suspected of kidnapping.

He also added a subplot and cut many scenes that slowed the story. While the film bombed in America, Chan's edited version held its own in the Asian market.

By this time, Chan was beginning to see a pattern in his American experiences. Each trip had taught him something new. He came to realize who he was as an actor and who he was not. He made a vow that if he ever went back to America to make a film, he wouldn't go back as Bruce Lee or Clint Eastwood. He would return only if he could be Jackie Chan.

Willie Chan agreed. But he had thought of a way to convince the determined Jackie that there were benefits to returning to the United States. He took stock of Chan's career, particularly the toll all the stunt work had taken on his body. Chan was certainly no stranger to injury. Almost every part of his body had been injured at one time or another. The stuntmen in his movies got so banged up that Golden Harvest couldn't get insurance for his shoots. And he had come close to a career-threatening injury that may very well have ended his life. While perfecting a shot for *Armor of God* in which he leaps from a ledge to a branch, Chan tumbled to the rocks below, suffering a serious head injury that required brain surgery. The countless falls, broken bones, neck injuries, and trips to the hospital would certainly shorten the young star's career if he kept up at his current rate. As usual, Willie had a plan.

A New Strategy

It was no secret that directors of American films relied on technologies such as blue screens and computer animation for stunt work. Blue screen animation works like this: the actor performs a "stunt" in front of a special blue screen. For instance, he or she may be wired above the set and pretend to fall. The scene is filmed, then superimposed on a background so it appears as though the actor is actually falling off a building or cliff.

Typically, American actors who play action heroes have more longevity because they fake the stunts. Willie suggested that Jackie learn these techniques in case there came the day when he would want to rely on them. Although he had

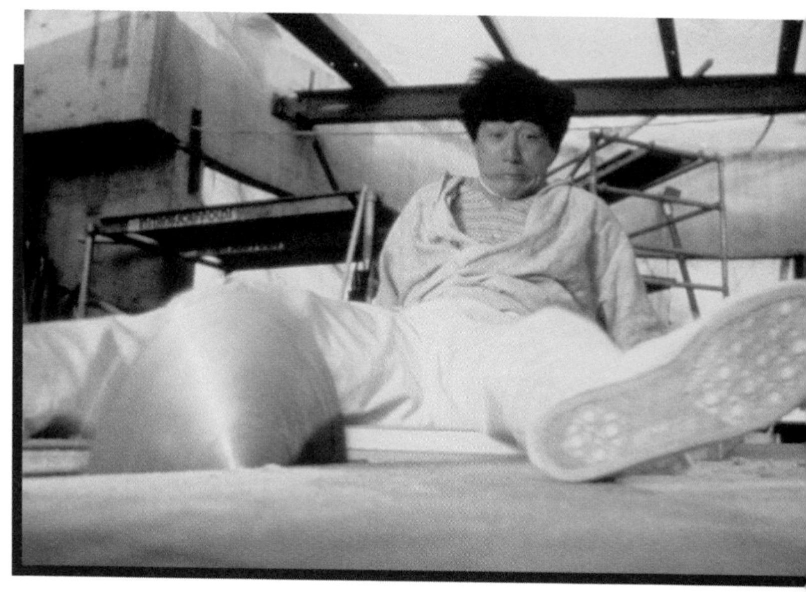

In *Mr. Nice Guy*, Jackie Chan stars as a TV cook who uses his martial arts skills to defend a journalist from drug thugs she videotaped committing murder.

always been opposed to such filmmaking shenanigans, Jackie saw Willie's point. So he began to look for the right role in Hollywood, one that would let him be Jackie Chan. He was offered projects by the likes of Sylvester Stallone, Wesley Snipes, and Bruce Willis. But all had him playing villains,

Jackie Chan *(right)* dons a skirt and a blond wig in a hilarious appearance on *Saturday Night Live.*

and he didn't think his fans in Hong Kong, Japan, and Thailand would want to see him getting thrashed, even by their American film heroes.

So he kept making films in Hong Kong while he continued the search for a role in America. Among the successes was *Rumble in the Bronx,* which incorporated a Western cast and location. This was part of an effort to make an "international" Hong Kong film. His old and trusted producers, Leonard Ho and Raymond Chow, believed the film could be Chan's ticket to the West. And they were right. For the third time, Chan packed his bags for America. Golden Harvest was on the verge of selling a package of his earlier films to U.S. distributors.

Rumble in the Bronx would help push the Jackie Chan phenomenon to American audiences. Chan was the benefactor of first-rate publicity. While he was making appearances on television and radio talk shows and posing for magazine covers, *Rumble* took in almost $10 million its opening weekend, making it the number one film in America.

Jackie Chan in *Shanghai Noon.* The movie presents a classic Western theme with a martial arts twist.

Finally, Chan was a hit with Americans. He was a real Hollywood movie star whose life's work was admired by thousands. All his hard work had paid off. The generosity of his friends, the advice of his elders, the bruises, breaks, and pain—everything finally clicked to make his dream come true. It was 1996, and America had discovered Jackie Chan.

Despite the list of injuries, the occasional debt, and the heartache that goes with sacrificing everything for a dream, Jackie Chan has emerged as a true hero, fit for moviegoers around the globe. And there is no stopping him now. Recent American smash hits such as *Shanghai Noon*, *Rush Hour*, and *Rush Hour 2* show the "man who can do anything" is not

Jackie Chan *(right)* and Chris Tucker star as a pair of detectives tracking down a murderous gang lord in the martial arts comedy *Rush Hour 2.*

about to slow down. With plans to produce a new movie every year, Jackie Chan will no doubt keep the dream of the dragon alive.

Filmography

Jackie Chan has appeared in the following films (under different stage names) as an actor, stuntman, stunt coordinator, director, or producer.

Big and Little Wong Tin Bar (1962)

The Lover Eternal (1963, aka: *Love Eterne*)

The Story of Qui Xiang Lin (1964)

Come Drink with Me (1966)

A Touch of Zen (1968)

Fist of Fury (1971, aka: *The Chinese Connection*)

The Little Tiger of Canton (1971, aka: *Master with Cracked Fingers*)

The Heroine (1971, aka: *Attack of the Kung Fu Girl*)

Police Woman (1971)

Hapkido (1972)

Not Scared to Die (1973, aka: *Eagle's Shadow Fist*)

Enter the Dragon (1973, aka: *The Deadly Three*)

The Young Dragons (1973)

Golden Lotus (1974)

The Himalayan (1975)

All in the Family (1975)

The Dragon Tamers (1975)

Hand of Death (1976, aka: *Countdown in Kung Fu*)

New Fist of Fury (1976)

Shaolin Wooden Men (1976)

Dance of Death (1976)

Iron Fisted Monk (1977)

Killer Meteor (1977, aka: *Jackie Chan vs. Wang Yu*)

To Kill with Intrigue (1977, aka: *Jackie Chan Connection*)

Snake and Crane Arts of Shaolin (1978)

Half a Loaf of Kung Fu (1978)

Magnificent Bodyguards (1978)

Spiritual Kung Fu (1978, aka: *Karate Ghost Buster)*

Dragon Fist (1978)

Snake in Eagle's Shadow (1978, aka: *Snaky Monkey*)

Drunken Master (1978, aka: *Drunk Monkey*)

Fearless Hyena (1979)

The 36 Crazy Fists (1979, aka: *Blood Pact)*

Fearless Hyena II (1980)

The Young Master (1980)

Battle Creek Brawl (1980, aka: *The Big Brawl*)

Cannonball Run (1980)

Dragon Lord (1982)

Fantasy Mission Force (1982, aka: *The Dragon Attack*)

Ninja Wars (1982)

Winners and Sinners (1983, aka: *Five Lucky Stars*)

Cannonball Run II (1983)

Project A (1984, aka: *Pirate Patrol*)

Wheels on Meals (1984)

Two in a Black Belt (1984)

Pom Pom (1984)

My Lucky Stars (1985)

Twinkle, Twinkle, Lucky Stars (1985)

The Protector (1985)

Heart of Dragon (1985, aka: *First Mission*)

Police Story (1985, aka: *Police Force*)

Armor of God (1986, aka: *Thunderarm*)

Naughty Boys (1986)

Project A II (1987, aka: *Project B*)

I Am Sorry (1987)

Dragons Forever (1987, aka: *Three Brothers*)

Police Story II (1988, aka: *Police Force II*)

Rouge (1988)

Inspector Wears Skirts (1989)

Outlaw Brothers (1989)

Miracles: Mr. Canton and Lady Rose (1989)

Stagedoor Johnny (1990)

Armor of God II: Operation Condor (1990)

Island on Fire (1991, aka: *When Dragons Meet, The Prisoner*)

Twin Dragons (1991, aka: *Double Dragons, Dragons Collide*)

A Kid from Tibet (1991)

Police Story III: Supercop (1992)

Actress (1993)

City Hunter (1993)

Project S (1993)

Crime Story (1993)

Drunken Master II (1994, aka: *Drunken Monkey II*)

Rumble in the Bronx (1994)

Thunderbolt (1995, aka: *Dead Heat*)

Police Story IV: First Strike (1996)

Mr. Nice Guy (1997, aka: *A Nice Guy*)

Burn Hollywood Burn: An Alan Smithee Film (1997)

Who Am I? (1998)

Rush Hour (1999)

Gorgeous (1999)

Gen X Cops (1999)

Shanghai Noon (2000)

Accidental Spy (2001)

Rush Hour 2 (2001)

Glossary

caning To hit or beat with a rod.

carte blanche The power to do whatever one wants.

ch'i The vital force of life.

entourage A group of attendants.

hapkido Korean martial art dating back to the fourteenth century.

indenture To bind someone to a service by contract.

inimitable One of a kind.

judo A Japanese sport similar to wrestling.

karate A traditional Japanese form of self-defense.

kung fu A broad term for many different types of Chinese martial arts.

lung fu mo shi ("dragon tiger") Chinese philosophy meaning extreme degrees of power, strength, and bravery.

parody Imitating a certain work of art, usually to a comic effect.

sifu Teacher.

For More Information

Web Sites

Already a Dragon: My Tribute to Jackie Chan Sing Lung, Already a Dragon
http://www.jackiechan.com

Golden Harvest Studios
http://www.goldenharvest.com

Jackie Chan Action Club
http://www.jackie-chan.com

Jackie Chan: The Movies
http://www.clapro.com/ekillian/jackie

Media Asia Group
http://www.mediaasia.com

People Are Strange
http://www.pkbaseline.com/screen/strange/people/chan/

Screen Power Publishing Group
Web site: www.screen-power.com

Video

The Deadliest Art: The Best of the Martial Arts Films. CBS/Fox Video, 1990.

For Further Reading

Chan, Jackie, and Jeff Yang. *I Am Jackie Chan: My Life in Action*. New York: Ballantine Books, 1998.

Gentry, Clyde, III. *Jackie Chan: Inside the Dragon*. Dallas, TX: Taylor Publishing, 1997.

Little, John R., and Curtis F. Wong, eds. *Jackie Chan*. Lincolnwood, IL: Contemporary Books, 1999.

Logan, Bey. *Hong Kong Action Cinema*. Woodstock, NY: Overlook Press, 1996.

Major, Wade. *Jackie Chan*. New York: Metrobooks, 1999.

Meyers, Richard. *Great Martial Arts Movies: From Bruce Lee to Jackie Chan and More.* Secaucus, NJ: Carol Publishing Group, 1999.

Rovin, Jeff, and Kathy Tracy. *The Essential Jackie Chan Sourcebook*. New York: Pocket Books, 1997.

Stokes, Lisa Odham, and Michael Hoover. *City on Fire: Hong Kong Cinema*. New York: Verso, 1999.

Teo, Stephen. *Hong Kong Cinema: The Extra Dimensions*. London: BFI, 1997.

Yau, Esther C. M., ed. *At Full Speed: Hong Kong Cinema in a Borderless World*. Minneapolis, MN: University of Minnesota Press, 2001.

Index

F

G

H

I

J

K

L

M

N

P

R

S

T

W

Y

About the Author

J. Poolos is a freelance writer and action film enthusiast who lives in Iowa.

Photo Credits

Cover, pp. 30, 35, 54–55, 63, 65, 70, 72, 74–75, 82–83, 85, 89, 90, 92, 94 © The Everett Collection; pp. 4–5 © Reuters NewMediaInc./Corbis; pp. 10, 20–21, 24 © Hulton/Archive by Getty Images; p. 13 © Liu Liqun/Corbis; p. 68 © AP/Wide World Photos.

Series Design and Layout

Les Kanturek